The purr-fect surprise

* * *

"Follow me," Hanni said, nudging Alfie toward the big kitchen, separated from the living area only by a gleaming white island. The Sobels' kitchen looked like a magazine picture, Alfie thought, but there wasn't any food lying around other than a big bowl of lemons. Alfie's mouth puckered up just thinking about them.

Why all the lemons?

Hanni was heading toward a sliding door at one side of the kitchen. "Surprise!" she said, pushing it open a little.

So Hanni had been teasing at the front door, Alfie thought, explaining it to herself. She could joke around! But here was the real surprise, in the laundry room. "*Kittens,*" she said, almost breathing out the word, she was so thrilled.

It was love at first sight.

Books by Sally Warner

* * *

THE ABSOLUTELY ALFIE SERIES

Absolutely Alfie and the Furry Purry Secret

Absolutely Alfie and the First Week Friends

Absolutely Alfie and the Worst Best Sleepover

THE ELLRAY JAKES SERIES

EllRay Jakes Is Not a Chicken!

EllRay Jakes Is a Rock Star!

EllRay Jakes Walks the Plank!

EllRay Jakes the Dragon Slayer!

EllRay Jakes and the Beanstalk

EllRay Jakes Is Magic!

EllRay Jakes Rocks the Holidays!

EllRay Jakes the Recess King!

EllRay Jakes Stands Tall!

THE EMMA SERIES

Only Emma

Not-So-Weird Emma

Super Emma

Best Friend Emma

Excellent Emma

ABSOLUTELY Alfie

and the FURRY PURRY SECRET

SALLY WARNER

illustrated by SHEARRY MALONE

PUFFIN BOOKS

PUFFIN BOOKS
An imprint of Penguin Random House LLC
375 Hudson Street
New York, New York 10014

Published simultaneously in the United States of America by Viking and Puffin Books,
imprints of Penguin Random House LLC, 2017

LIBRARY OF CONGRESS CATALOGING-IN-PUBLICATION DATA IS AVAILABLE

Puffin Books ISBN 9781101999882

Printed in the United States of America
Book design by Nancy Brennan

3 5 7 9 10 8 6 4 2

To Della Sutherland—S.W.

To my sister. This is for you, Lynn.
Without your unwavering love and support,
this would not have been possible.
I love you. —S.M.

Contents

ABSOLUTELY Alfie

and the FURRY PURRY SECRET

Floop!

"It's the last three weeks of summer, and there's absolutely nothing to do," Alfie Jakes said to her mom one Sunday night in early August. "I'm eight years old. I'm missing out on all the fun in life!" She drooped onto the kitchen island like a comma to show how sad she was. She shoved her hand against the island so she could whirl around in one of the tall chairs.

Getting dizzy was *something* cool to do, anyway—when every other summer activity had come to an end.

Little Acorns Daycamp, where she had woven the world's blobbiest potholder.

Tumbling lessons at Oak Glen Parks and Rec.

Swim lessons at the Y.

Alfie liked keeping busy.

But now, even the Jakeses' family vacation to San Francisco was long gone, along with the funny burnt-toast smell of that city's cable cars, its foggy summer mornings, and the thrill of shopping for souvenirs in Chinatown. So cool.

Alfie *loved* souvenirs. She thought regular life should have souvenirs—every single day. Why not? "Yes, it was just a boring Sunday in August. But I bought the cutest T-shirt to remember it by!"

Alfie definitely wanted to live in San Francisco when she grew up. It had to be the best place in the world. It was much more fun than Oak Glen, California, for sure. So *that* was settled, she told herself, getting ready for another spin.

"Don't be so dramatic, Miss Alfie," her mom said, laughing. "First, you're only seven years old," she reminded her daughter. "You won't be eight until November. Second, you had a lovely summer. And third, don't twirl around like that, sweetie. It's distracting, and it's hard on the chair." Mrs. Jakes stirred the pot on the stove with a wooden spoon held in one hand. Her other hand marked a spot partway through whatever recipe she was trying to follow.

Alfie's mom did not like to cook, especially in summer. She would much rather be working on one of her books about the olden days, Alfie knew. Her mother's first book had appeared in bookstores a year ago, and even Alfie and her big brother EllRay knew that was a big deal. But Alfie's mom was now hard at work on *another* book. That surprised Alfie. She had already written one, hadn't she?

Was that what being a grown-up was like, doing the same thing over and over again?

Boo!

Her own life was going to much more exciting, Alfie promised herself. If her mom wasn't writing, she liked being outside—working in the garden or doing something fun. Just like Alfie. Mrs. Jakes and Alfie had fun in common.

"My good-time girls," Alfie's dad called them, joking. He also called Alfie "Cricket," because she was so small and energetic, and she could jump really, really far.

"I know I'm seven," Alfie said, her voice a grumble. "I was just practicing."

"Are you telling me you're bored?" her mother asked, glancing over at her.

Alfie hesitated. She and EllRay had learned long ago what happened if they complained to their mom or dad that they were bored. "You make your own life interesting," their parents would remind the two kids. "But there are plenty of chores that need doing if you run out of ideas. Just let us know."

"I'm not exactly *bored,*" Alfie told her mom now, sounding cautious.

Mrs. Jakes laughed, as if she'd been teasing. She was a pretty mom with a nice smile and short, curly hair she often wore tied back with a colorful scarf. "Look," she said, turning off the burner on the stove. "I know this is 'The Vacuum,' Alfie, the time when summer is almost over. You're basically just hanging around, waiting for school to start. On the twenty-eighth," she added.

She would be in second grade, Alfie reminded herself, her breath catching in her throat. With a new teacher, Mr. Havens. A *boy* teacher. There would be new kids to meet, too.

Her tummy gave a funny little jump. *Floop!*

"'The Vacuum?'" Alfie asked her mom. "You mean like a vacuum cleaner?"

"Not exactly," her mom

said. "The word *vacuum* comes from the Latin word meaning *empty*, Alfie. I was trying to say that we're in kind of an empty period, here."

"But it's *real time*," Alfie argued, trying not to think of the first day of school. "And it's in my real life, Mom. There are three whole weeks of summer left, and they should count just as much as any other weeks. Do you want to hurt those weeks' feelings? A person can fly around the world in three weeks, EllRay told me once—and even see stuff along the way."

"Well, I'm not going to fly you around the world, tempting as that sounds," her mother said, laughing again. "But Mrs. Sobel and I were talking on the phone yesterday. We're in the same situation, it seems, since we both work at home."

Mrs. Sobel was Hanni Sobel's mother. The Sobels had moved to Oak Glen a year ago and lived only one block away.

Alfie and Hanni had been in first grade together, but they were not first-best-friends or even second-best-friends. They didn't exactly have a lot in common, in Alfie's opinion. She was a fun-loving cricket, and Hanni was "the world's oldest seven-year-old," to quote Alfie's mom.

In other words, Hanni Sobel was kind of a know-it-all who tried to be the boss of the other girls.

"We came up with something that might be fun for you and Hanni," Alfie's mom was saying.

"Like what?" Alfie asked, suddenly nervous.

"Like a two-girl daycare club," Mrs. Jakes said. "One day at our house, and the next day at Hanni's house, and so on. From nine in the morning until three in the afternoon each day, Monday through Friday, for the next three weeks. There's even a small budget for craft supplies and special activities," she added, knowing this would grab Alfie's attention. "We think we can count on you girls to organize your own activities in a fun but sensible way," she said.

That probably meant no TV, Alfie knew. And very limited time for video games, if any. But—craft supplies! Craft supplies were nearly as good as souvenirs. Alfie could almost smell the paste and feel small glittery stickers decorating her fingertips.

Alfie Jakes was a champion shopper. For fun stuff, anyway.

"Does Hanni know about this?" Alfie asked, her

tummy fluttering again—because she didn't want the would-be boss of the girls to end up being her enemy by the time school began.

Alfie wanted second grade to get off to a really good start.

"Hanni's all for it," Alfie's mom reported.

She *was*?

"So when do we begin?" Alfie asked. Her brown eyes were wide with excitement.

"Tomorrow morning. Nine A.M. sharp. Our house," Mrs. Jakes said, smiling at the success of her plan. "So start thinking of some fun things the two of you can do, Alfie. And then you, Hanni, and I will go shopping for craft supplies tomorrow afternoon, before it's time for Hanni to go home. That way you'll each get to choose some things you like."

"I can't wait," Alfie said, hopping off the kitchen stool. "I'm gonna go start a list right now!"

That end-of-summer vacuum was filling up—*fast*.

Playing Ping-Pong with Words

"So what game is it gonna be tonight?" EllRay asked Alfie after dinner as they sprawled on the rug in his room. Sunday night board games were a brother-sister tradition in the Jakes household. "B-o-r-e-d" games, EllRay sometimes teased, spelling it out. Alfie didn't really get the joke at first.

Mrs. Jakes even made a special Sunday night snack for the kids to share.

"Hmm," Alfie said, thinking about it.

EllRay was eleven years old. He was a tall, skinny string bean of a boy, their mom often said when describing him. But Alfie knew from family stories that he'd been the shortest kid in his class when he was her age. Now he was obsessed with sports and his friends, but he still hung out with Alfie sometimes. They were a team.

She was the shortest kid in *her* class last year, she reminded herself, but that wasn't so bad, because she was a girl. Her dad would still carry her in from the car at night if she pretended to be asleep.

She loved that.

"I don't know what game. You decide," Alfie said, still damp from her summer evening shower. Her lavender tank top and pink-and-white-striped jammie bottoms felt soft against her golden brown skin. She could still smell that night's strawberry shortcake in the air.

"No. You decide," he said.

"You decide."

"You decide."

"No, you," Alfie insisted.

Her brother reached for a nearby stack of games with a long brown arm. "Well, you got your candy game, where you hop along the path," he announced, like he was selling it at the county fair.

The fair had been the end of fun for their family that summer, Alfie remembered. But the two-girl daycare club was going to fix *that*. If it worked out, anyway.

Craft supplies!

"And you got your operation game," EllRay continued, still being the salesman. "You know, where the goofy guy's nose lights up and the buzzer sounds when you make a mistake. Except you like to do that on purpose, Alfie. And it messes up the whole thing," he complained. "And then you got that game where you always lose your temper and throw the pieces across the room. Except I'm not sure we still have all the pieces—for obvious reasons, *Alfleta*," he added, making a funny face.

"Alfleta" was her long name, one her mom had once used in a book. It meant "beautiful elf" in some old language no one spoke anymore.

"Stop teasing," Alfie commanded. "I choose the candy game."

"*For ages three and up*," EllRay said, reading aloud from the box. "That sounds about right."

"Quit it," Alfie told him. "It's fun, and you know it."

"It's okay," EllRay said, shrugging. He unfolded the colorful board and reached for a massive handful of popcorn.

Alfie straightened the stack of cards and set up two figures for them to use. "You're red, I'm green," she informed her brother. "And I get to go first because I'm the littlest. Maybe I'll play this game tomorrow when Hanni Sobel comes over," she added, like the visit was no big deal. "I can get good at it tonight, then wipe her out."

"Nice," EllRay said, laughing. "There's not a whole lot of strategy to this game, though, Alf. And how come Hanni's coming over? Does someone in this house need bossing around?"

"She's not that bad," Alfie said. "And she's coming over to fix the vacuum," she explained, drawing the first card.

Blue. She bounced her green plastic figure forward until it reached a blue square.

"What vacuum? And you don't have to actually hit each square when you move," EllRay told his sister, shaking his head. "You can just find the right color with your eyeballs and put your piece there."

"You play your way, and I'll play my way," Alfie said.

"But it gets on my nerves when you go *click-click-click* all the time," EllRay said, picking a

card and then moving his red figure forward—without touching the board on the way.

"And it gets on *my* nerves when you chew popcorn with your mouth open while you tell me what to do," Alfie replied.

They weren't really fighting. It was more like playing Ping-Pong with words.

It was a brother-and-sister thing.

"But I remember Hanni Sobel from last year at school," EllRay said, stretching while he waited. "She thinks she knows everything. And that's gonna be rough, because you know everything, too," he teased. "Your turn to pick a card."

"Yeah, but she really kinda does know everything," Alfie explained, examining her new card.

"This says I'm supposed to lose one turn," she said, flapping the card in the air as if it smelled bad and waving it might help. "But I don't think it really means that."

EllRay sighed again. "You decide what you want to do with it, then," he said. "Because I'm not gonna fight about it. But is that what you're going to say to Hanni tomorrow when you get that card? That you want to play the baby way?"

"Maybe I will, and maybe I won't," Alfie said.

She liked this kind of reply. It made it harder to be wrong.

"*That* gets on my nerves, too," EllRay said, shaking his head. "*Maybe this, but maybe that*. It's kind of what you say about everything lately."

"Maybe I do, and maybe I don't," Alfie replied. "But okay, EllRay. Have it your way. I'll lose one turn. And I'm *not a baby*."

"Maybe you are, and maybe you're not," EllRay said with a grin. "I guess we'll find out tomorrow when Hanni Sobel gets here. Right?"

"Maybe we will, and maybe we won't," Alfie told him.

Ha!

Backwards Day

Alfie was so excited the next morning that she couldn't think straight. What should she and Hanni do first? She only had two more hours to figure it out!

"How does this sound?" she asked her mom between messy bites of her breakfast burrito. Ell-Ray had already disappeared outside with his. "I'm thinking we can start with dolls, unless Hanni thinks they're too babyish. And then maybe we'll have a tea party," she said. Tea parties were a good excuse to eat cookies. And who didn't like eating cookies?

Alfie's mom was careful about snacks, but she'd be busy working on her book.

"And then we can go outside and play for half

an hour," Alfie continued. "And maybe make hand puppets, only with new socks, because otherwise it's just gross. Too many smelly feet-ghosts in old socks," she explained, shuddering. "And then I'll tell Hanni about our vacation. Then—"

"Hold on a minute," Mrs. Jakes said, putting down her cup of tea. "You're not a cruise director or a camp counselor, sweetie. This three-week day-care club is supposed to be relaxing and fun for both of you. So how about asking Hanni what *she* would like to do? Just regular hanging-out things, Alfie."

"But I've never really played with Hanni at school," Alfie admitted. "Not just the two of us, Mom. She's usually busy solving other kids' problems or telling them what to do. And I'm usually running around playing."

"You must have *some* things in common that you like to do," her mom said.

"Not really," Alfie replied, shaking her head. "And if Hanni gets bored here, she might not want to hang out with me by the time school begins," she added, frowning. "She might tell the new kids

I'm boring. And then second grade will get off to a terrible start. So my *entire life* depends on how things go today."

Alfie had decided over the summer that the start of each new school year was like an imaginary whiteboard that had been wiped clean. True, there were still faint traces on it of things that had been written before, or that had happened before. But it was mostly blank.

And she was excited about the idea of starting out fresh. She could be anything!

"No it doesn't, Miss Drama Queen," her mom said, laughing. "Don't go giving yourself stage fright for no reason. This is just another Monday morning, only you have a friend—a *new* friend, apparently—coming over to play. And then you girls will get to go shopping. Period. So stop making such a big deal out of this."

Huh, Alfie thought, scowling some more as she finished her burrito. That was easy for her mom to say.

She didn't really get it.

❋ ❋ ❋

Mrs. Sobel walked Hanni over to the Jakeses' house, even though the Sobels only lived a block away. "No walking alone," the parents had decided.

"Hey," Hanni said, sliding a glance toward Alfie when the front door opened. Alfie hoped her softly twisted pigtails looked as cute this morning as they usually did.

Hanni Sobel's hair looked good. She had wavy dark hair, green eyes, and a narrow face that dimpled when she smiled. But—*uh-oh,* Alfie thought. Hanni did not look happy. What was up with that?

"Someone got up on the wrong side of the bed this morning, Louise," Mrs. Sobel told Alfie's mom, pretend-whispering. Mrs. Sobel was a comfortably rounded woman with a broad smile and a haircut that seemed to be all straight lines, Alfie noted. Maybe she used a ruler when she cut it.

"She got up on the wrong side of the bed" was an expression that meant Hanni was in a bad mood, Alfie knew.

Great.

"But I always get up on the same side," Hanni pointed out. "I get up on the *right* side, Mom."

Pure Hanni.

"I just meant you aren't your usual sunny self, as you very well know," Mrs. Sobel explained, laughing. "But you can just turn that frown upside-down, missy," she added, refusing to be anything but cheerful as she prepared to leave. "It's a beautiful day, and you're going to have a wonderful time with Alfie."

An okay day and a so-so time would be enough to hope for at this point, Alfie thought. Yesterday's tummy flutters returned as she peeked at Hanni's stony face.

"I'm sorry you got up on the wrong side of the bed," Alfie said to Hanni once they were alone in Alfie's room. "Is there any cure for that?"

"Nope," Hanni said, looking around.

"Too bad," Alfie said.

"So sad."

And they laughed together for the first time. Hanni's dimple appeared.

Alfie had hidden away a couple of toys she didn't want to share, but she had scattered other fun things around the room in what she hoped was a tempting way.

Her metal box full of stickers.

The candy board game.

A basketful of small dolls wearing very cool clothes.

"Maybe I can trick myself out of my bad mood by doing stuff exactly the opposite?" Hanni said, coming up with the idea *just like that.* "Not cure getting out of bed, because that already happened," she explained. "But everything else."

"We should do stuff backwards today," Alfie said, playing with the beaded end of one of her pig-tails. "We could even try *walking* backwards, if we can do it without falling over."

"Maybe not walking backwards down the stairs," Hanni cautioned, her hair growing springier and more cheerful with each word. "But around the block? Everyone will think we're so goofy and weird!"

"It'll be absolutely great," Alfie said, picturing her neighbors' expressions—if anyone was outside on such a hot August day. "But we gotta put our clothes on backwards first," she said, daring to make the suggestion. "Otherwise, the trick might not work."

Switching their clothes around was easy to do, since it was a shorts-and-T-shirt summer day. Two minutes later, their shorts pooched out in front where their bottoms used to be, and T-shirt labels tickled their throats instead of the backs of their necks. But they still looked cute. "Let's go, *Eifla*," Hanni said. "That's 'Alfie' spelled backwards," she explained. "It'll be our secret code for Backwards Day."

Hanni Sobel could spell backwards in her head.

"Um, okay, *Innah*," Alfie replied, feeling proud of herself—and relieved that Hanni's name was so short. "I gotta tell Mom we're going out, but she'll say yes. As long as we stick together and only walk one block."

"And if we see your big brother," Hanni-*Innah* said, "we're calling him *YarLle*. You know, instead of EllRay," she explained.

EllRay was going to be a sixth-grader at Oak

Glen, so Hanni already knew him.

Hanni was *amazing,* figuring out his backwards name that fast.

"It makes him sound like an alien from *Star Wars,*" Alfie said, smiling. "It's perfect."

"*I'm* perfect," Hanni said, probably half teasing, Alfie thought.

"Maybe you are, and maybe you aren't," she said with a matching smile.

"I *are,*" Hanni insisted, making a face.

"If you say so."

"So let's go, backwards girl," Hanni said with a grin on her face that had, in fact, turned her frown upside-down. "And when we get home, maybe we can do other stuff backwards, too. Like un-make your bed, and switch all your dolls' clothes around."

"And eat our dessert first at lunch," Alfie chimed in.

"So let's get going, *Eifla,*" Hanni said again, whirling around to show off her backwards outfit. "This is gonna be a really fun day!"

And tomorrow would be another one, Alfie thought happily.

What a *relief.*

Surprise!

"C'mon in," Hanni said to Alfie the next morning at nine A.M. sharp, opening her front door a tiny crack. "Only don't let any of them out."

"Any of who? Any of what?" Alfie asked. Hanni was still such a mystery that she could be talking about anything! For all Alfie knew, the Sobels were raising butterflies in their living room.

Or maybe they had a lizard ranch in there.

But this was a pretty cool way for a Tuesday in August to start.

"I'm in," Alfie said, slipping through the door. She looked around, curious. Her own house was comfortable and pretty, with lots of bright colors, books, and beautiful rocks on display, since Alfie's dad was a geology professor at a college in San Diego. But the Sobels' house was modern, sleek, and shiny. There were no butterflies or lizards in sight.

"I like your house," Alfie told Hanni, feeling shy.

"It's okay," Hanni said, looking around with a doubtful shrug. "Only we can't make a mess, except in my room. That's where I'm keeping the craft supplies."

After a successful shopping trip the previous afternoon, the girls had divided their loot into two bags in the back of Mrs. Jakes's car.

"Can I see your room?" Alfie asked.

"Yeah, but I wanna show you something else first," Hanni said. "*That's my mom's office,*" she added, whispering the words as they passed a partly open door.

"Hello, Alfie," Mrs. Sobel sang out from behind the door.

"Hi, Mrs. Sobel," Alfie called back. "Thanks for having me over."

"No problem!"

Whenever somebody said "No problem," Alfie always thought there probably *was* a problem, she just didn't know what it was yet.

"Follow me," Hanni said, nudging Alfie toward the big kitchen, separated from the living area only by a gleaming white island. The Sobels' kitchen looked like a magazine picture, Alfie thought, but there wasn't any food lying around other than a big bowl of lemons. Alfie's mouth puckered up just thinking about them.

Why all the lemons?

Hanni was heading toward a sliding door at one side of the kitchen. "Surprise!" she said, pushing it open a little.

So Hanni had been teasing at the front door, Alfie thought, explaining it to herself. She could joke around! But here was the real surprise, in the laundry room. *"Kittens,"* she said, almost breathing out the word, she was so thrilled.

It was love at first sight.

Alfie Jakes had wanted a kitten for as long as she could remember. But her mom was convinced that Alfie was allergic to animal fur.

And that meant *"No Pets."*

It was an official family rule.

"I had a stuffy nose when I was two, Mom," Alfie had tried to argue more than once. "And yes, *maybe* I was around somebody's cat or dog when it happened. But that doesn't mean I'm allergic."

"You're healthy when you're *not* around cats and dogs," Mrs. Jakes always pointed out.

"But I'd probably be healthy anyway," Alfie argued. "I'm a healthy kid!"

"Kittens," Alfie said again now, feeling as though she had walked into some wonderful cartoon.

5

Free to a Good Home

The black mama cat—Domino—had white spots on her chest and tummy. She sprawled in a splash of sunshine in a blanket-lined basket. There was a sleepy, pleased look on her face as she watched her three kittens play.

The kittens were the cutest things Alfie had ever seen, not counting videos of baby goats on the Internet. "They're *beautiful,* Hanni," Alfie said, sinking to her knees on the shiny laundry room floor.

"Thought you'd like them," Hanni said in a satisfied way, sliding the door shut behind them. She sat down next to Alfie and twiddled her fingers on the floor to get the kittens' attention.

"I thought kitties' eyes were always shut," Alfie said, staring at the little animals in a hungry way.

She wanted a kitten—big-time.

And she especially wanted the gray kitty who looked like it was wearing a little white vest.

Love *on top of* love at first sight.

"Yeah. Their eyes are shut when they're first born," Hanni informed her. "And their ears are kind of pasted down, too. But these guys are almost eight weeks old. They've already had their shots. They're gonna leave pretty soon. Two of them, anyway."

Leave? But where would they go? Alfie pictured two kittens packing tiny suitcases or duffel bags and tottering out the Sobels' wide front door.

She knew that wasn't what really happened, but it was fun to imagine it.

"Domino had these kittens by accident," Hanni was explaining. "See, we never had a girl cat before, and my mom didn't know Domino could have kittens before she was one year old, even. But all of a sudden, *kittens*. Mom says *that's* never happening again," she added, sounding a little sad.

“Huh,” Alfie said. The Jakes family had never had a pet, so Alfie wasn’t really sure what Hanni was talking about. But she didn’t want Hanni to know that.

Two of the kitties were sitting up very straight, as if they’d been told to pay attention in class. The third kitten, Alfie’s favorite—the one who looked like it was wearing striped socks and a white vest—had puffed itself up and was hopping sideways toward the other two. It was probably pretending to be scary, Alfie thought, smiling again. Then the hopping kitten saw Hanni’s moving fingers. It crouched, its waggling rear end in the air, preparing to pounce.

Adorable.

And Alfie's nose wasn't running the tiniest little bit!

See? She *wasn't* allergic to animal fur. Especially not to *this* animal's fur.

"Hold it," Hanni urged, and so Alfie scooped up the crouching kitten as if she'd done it every day of her life.

The kitten nestled against Alfie's T-shirt and started to purr. "It likes me," Alfie said, thrilled. She could almost see sparkles in the air and hear pink and blue cartoon birds start to sing.

"That's the kitty who doesn't have a home," Hanni said, shaking her head. "Poor little thing."

"You're really not gonna keep it?" Alfie asked, amazed. If they were her kittens, she'd keep them all!

"Mom says no," Hanni said. "I already asked."

"So, someone else will get to take it home," Alfie said, thinking aloud.

"I guess," Hanni said, shrugging. "In a week. And it's a girl kitty, by the way."

"Are kittens expensive?" Alfie asked. Her mind was starting to whir. She had fourteen dollars saved up for emergency spending. The money was hidden in her ballerina jewelry box.

This was definitely an emergency. But would fourteen dollars be enough?

"Some of 'em are expensive," Hanni said. "But this kitty is 'free to a good home,' my mom says."

Wow, Alfie thought, amazed. *Free.* Free was the perfect price!

Wait a minute, she told herself suddenly, her eyes wide. What was she thinking? She didn't have permission to bring a kitten home.

It wasn't fair!

The Decision

Two days later, on Thursday, Oak Glen was in the middle of a real heat wave. When it started to cool down that evening, Alfie and EllRay went outside after dinner to play. A yellow plastic water slide stretched across the back lawn in the fading light. A hose dribbled nearby on the soggy grass.

Alfie Jakes was famous in her family for not being able to keep a secret. Even when someone was opening a present, she often blurted out what was inside.

"It's hiking boots!"

"It's a sweater!"

"It's a new skateboard!"

She liked being an expert on *something,* even if she was only seven. And spilling the beans about a gift was almost as good as buying the present herself, in Alfie's opinion. So it was hard keeping a secret about an *actual kitten* that she was desperately hoping would come to live in their very own house, if Alfie's wish came true. She shivered in anticipation as she got ready for her first slippery turn on the water slide.

You had to be careful with water slides, Alfie reminded herself as she crouched, getting ready to make her run. If there was a dry spot on the plastic, you might screech to a halt on it, and that stung like crazy.

"Is the slide totally wet?" Alfie called out to her brother, waggling her bottom a little as she prepared to make her dash.

"Of course it is," he shouted back. "Just go."

"You better not be kidding me, EllRay, or you'll be sorry," Alfie said.

She crouched again, stalling.

The kitty would have to be kept a secret at first. That was her new plan.

But she was right about not being allergic, Alfie thought, doing a couple of improvised pre-slide stretches. And having a new kitty would make her feel better about starting school with a boy teacher. Feel better about everything. She'd be the girl with the cute gray kitten at home.

That would be the first mark on her imaginary second grade whiteboard.

When the kitten was ready, Alfie thought, her heart pounding, she would sneak it home from Hanni's house and straight to her room. Maybe even next week! And by the time her family found out, she—still sniffle-free—would be able to prove she wasn't allergic to animal fur.

Yes, she would be breaking a family rule.

Yes, she might get in trouble.

Okay, she'd *for sure* get in trouble.

But the rule was wrong!

The actual kitty-sneaking wouldn't be too hard, if she really did it, Alfie assured herself. The gray kitten was tiny, not much bigger than a cupcake. Alfie would tuck her under a baggy T-shirt and just do it.

Alfie could picture the whole thing. She would hurry the kitten upstairs once she got home. She'd shut the door to her room—after hanging up the glittery *Privacy, Please!* sign she had made at Hanni's house during a lively craft afternoon.

Earlier that summer, she and her mother had made a deal that if Alfie could keep her room clean, her mom wouldn't keep inspecting it all the time.

But how long would she be able to keep the kitten a secret from the rest of her family? A couple of weeks, probably, Alfie assured herself. At least until school got started at the end of August. By then, she would be the proud owner of a perfectly trained kitten—who might even be able to do tricks!

Could kittens learn how to do tricks?

"Hey, it's almost dark. I'm falling asleep over here," EllRay yelled, sounding just about fed up. "I want a turn, too, you know. Are you going to slide, or are you just gonna stand there like a statue?" he asked, his hands on his hips.

"*You're* the statue," Alfie replied.

"No. You are," EllRay said.

"No, you," Alfie said. "I'm going to slide so far that I'll shoot off the end and just keep flying," she announced, backing up for the best head start ever.

And she *did* fly off the water slide! In fact, Alfie's wet skin ended up coated with so many tiny grass clippings that her brother couldn't stop laughing. "You're totally covered, Alf," he finally said, gasping. "It was worth the wait. Porcupine," he added, pointing.

"Not a porcupine," Alfie said, laughing too. "Call me a kitty instead, okay?"

She was dying to tell EllRay her big—make that *huge*—idea.

In fact, she was *this close* to doing it—but she kept her mouth shut. For now.

And EllRay hosed the grass bits off her so they could play outside a while longer. Then they went inside for their dessert.

Chocolate pudding.

Just before bedtime, Alfie sidled into her big brother's room. He was lying stomach-down on his bed, reading.

"What comic book is that?" she asked, settling down cross-legged on the rug next to his bed.

"It's a graphic novel, not a comic book," EllRay informed her.

"Big difference," Alfie said.

"There *is* a big difference, for your information," EllRay told her. "*You* don't know."

"Neither do you," she told him.

"And neither do you," EllRay said.

"Okay, okay," she said, tired of silly-arguing with him. "But I wanted to ask you something. Did you ever wish we had a pet when you were little?"

This was the perfect way of getting his opinion about her kitty idea, she had decided. "Sounding someone out," her dad called it. That meant getting another person's opinion about something you were thinking of doing.

"Sure I did," EllRay said, not looking up. "But you're allergic, so we never could. '*No Pets*,' remember?"

"Mom *says* I'm allergic," Alfie pointed out. "Only I don't think I really am. Not anymore. And anyway, we should get to decide what rules make sense around here or not."

"Since when?" EllRay asked, laughing.

"Since now."

"Fine," EllRay said, still trying to read. "Have it your way. Make up your own rules as you go along, and see how that goes down."

"But aren't you *lonely* for a pet?" she asked, trying another angle. She fluffed up the rug's tufts of wool with her fingers to make them prettier.

"Nah," he said, laughing. "I've got you, haven't I? It's enough trouble around here taking care of you, Alf. Feeding you treats. Training you not to make messes. Taking you for nice long walks."

"Be quiet," Alfie told him, since she was not allowed to say *"Shut up."*

But she was laughing, too.

"Who do *I* have to take care of, though?" she asked, sneaking in the serious question between giggles. "Who do I get to love?"

"Huh?"

"Oh, nothing," Alfie said.

"Once school starts," EllRay told her, "you won't have time to worry about not having a pet, or about being allergic to stuff. Coach Havens is probably gonna be a really strict teacher. He's a pretty tough coach. Good, but tough."

Oh yeah, Alfie thought—Mr. Havens. She'd forgotten all about him.

That's what even the *idea* of a kitty could do for a girl.

Fix just about anything!

And that's when Alfie made up her mind.

Yes, she *could* ask her mom and dad for permission to bring the kitten home, Alfie reminded herself. But once you asked for something big at her house, the discussions began.

Family meetings.

Pros and cons.

"Cooling-off periods," even. That meant *waiting.*

Alfie hated waiting.

And if she waited too long, this perfect kitten—*her kitten*—might end up going home with someone else!

Unacceptable, as Dad might say.

Yes, her mom and dad would get mad at her when they found out. Or worse, be disappointed in her. But life could be fair once, anyway—even if she had to break a family rule to make it fair. This kitten—"Princess," Alfie decided instantly—needed her.

"Operation Kittycat," she would call it, as if her kitten-smuggling plan was the plot of one of her dad's TV series about a spy or a bank robber.

But this was going to be real. Alfie absolutely needed for it to happen.

And the decision was *all hers.*

She would call Hanni tonight and tell her the good news.

"I'll take her!"

Kitten School

Alfie went to Hanni's house the following Tuesday. She hoped like anything that she would somehow be able to sneak Princess home with her on Thursday, two days later.

Operation Kittycat.

Today, however, Hanni Sobel had plans. "It's Kitten School day," she told Alfie when they had settled on the laundry room floor. The scent of fabric softener floated in the air. Their legs sprawled in the sunlight that streamed through the room's big windows.

"Well, Princess is not a very good meow-er yet," Alfie admitted, watching the three kittens play. "Maybe we could start with that." She cleared her throat as if preparing to let out a meow or two.

"I meant I'm teaching *you*," Hanni said, laughing.

"I knew that," Alfie said. "I was kidding." She felt her cheeks get hot.

Hanni probably knew a lot about kitties, Alfie thought, biting her lip as she prepared for the lesson. Hanni had firm opinions about everything, it seemed. She had even given Alfie advice on doing her hair last Friday!

"I think those twisted knot thingies that stick up would look really cute on you," Hanni had informed Alfie that day. "Or maybe a mixture of tight braids and puffballs."

Bantu knots. Cornrows. Afro puffs, Alfie thought now, frowning as she remembered. Not that any of that was Hanni's business. After all, she was white! Alfie was the one with brown skin.

And her mom did her hair. She was the expert.

What made Hanni such a hair wizard, anyway? It wasn't like *hers* was so spectacular!

But Alfie had decided not to tell her mom about Hanni's random hair advice. She knew the story would not go over very well, and she wanted this two-girl daycare thing—this *kitten* thing!—to work. Also, she was starting to like Hanni Sobel a lot in spite of all her opinions and advice.

Hanni laughed at her jokes—and she had a great laugh.

Hanni was also a good sharer, and she let Alfie play with anything she wanted.

Hanni even told Alfie she had good ideas about things to do. "You're a good thinker-upper, Alfie," she had said.

It would be cool heading into second grade with a brand-new friend, even if she could be a little bossy at times.

But maybe nobody was perfect.

"Okay. Kitten School," Alfie repeated, staring at the kittens.

Princess was washing herself as if she'd been doing it for ages, Alfie noted, watching her future kitty in action. First, Princess turned her little round head and licked each striped shoulder with great care. She tried to lick her white vest without much luck. Then she licked a paw, swiping it behind her furry ear and making it go *boing*.

Alfie wasn't sure, but she didn't think human

babies could take care of themselves that fast in life. She felt *proud* of Princess.

Maybe she was a kitten genius!

Wouldn't it be cool if Princess could learn to count—or even say something?

"I love you," maybe. Alfie would get EllRay to make a video of it for YouTube, getting carried away with the idea. They could even add some music. And they'd post it.

She and Princess would be famous!

"Pay attention," Hanni said, sounding very

stern. “Lesson number one,” she began, scooching her bottom over toward the litter box. “You gotta clean the poops out of the litter box every single day. And you have to change all the litter at least once a week, and scrub the box, too. Because of the wee-wee,” she explained.

Huh?

Alfie made a face as her dream of YouTube fame flew out the window. “How do you get the poops out of the box?” she asked, not having pictured any of these icky details.

Princess was pretty small, though. And worth it, Alfie hoped.

“The poops kind of turn into clumps, because of the litter,” Hanni explained. “And you just scoop them out, or use little plastic bags.” She waved a slotted yellow plastic pooper-scooper in the air to demonstrate the first method of poop removal.

Another thing to buy, Alfie thought. She pictured her painfully saved-up fourteen dollars disappearing like so many bursting soap bubbles.

Or maybe she could just sneak a big spoon out of the kitchen and use that?

“You put the poops into a plastic bag, close it

tight, and throw it in the trash," Hanni was saying. "Never flush any of it, or the plumber will have to come, and you'll be sorry."

"Never flush any of it," Alfie repeated, robot-like.

"Okay. Now, feeding," Hanni continued. "I'll give you a little bag of litter and some kitten chow to get you started," she said as if she were crossing things off an invisible list. "But you gotta use the small kind, or she might choke."

Duh, Alfie thought, fiddling with one of her pigtails. But she didn't say it aloud, because Princess wasn't officially her kitty yet. If she made a fuss, Alfie thought, Hanni might change her mind about giving her away. "What about milk?" she asked instead, offering Hanni another chance to be the teacher. "Kitties like milk, don't they?"

"Well, do you like chocolate milkshakes?" Hanni asked.

"Yeah, sure," Alfie said.

"Does that mean you drink chocolate milkshakes all the time?" Hanni asked. "For breakfast, lunch, and dinner?"

Whoo, Hanni could be kind of a pain, Alfie thought, wincing. "Absolutely not," she said, mostly because she knew that was the correct answer.

But she wouldn't mind *trying* to drink chocolate milkshakes all the time.

"See?" Hanni said, as if she had just finished teaching a lesson.

"I don't get it," Alfie said. "You're saying kitties *don't* like milk?"

"It doesn't matter if they like it," Hanni explained. "I'm saying don't give your new kitty cow milk, or she might poo all over the floor."

Gak!

If that ever happened, Alfie thought, there was *no way* she could keep Princess a secret from her parents. Or even from EllRay. Her mom's nose was a super-sniffer when it came to bad smells in the house.

"Would it hurt someone to take out the trash?" Mrs. Jakes sometimes said.

"EllRay! Dirty socks in the hamper right away, please. '*Clean Up Your Mess,*'" she might add, quoting another family rule.

"So what will my kitty drink?" Alfie asked Hanni.

"Water," Hanni said—as if now, she was the one thinking *Duh*.

"Okay, water," Alfie said. "And what about brushing her hair?"

"It's called 'fur' on cats, not hair," Hanni said, ever the expert. "And you do it really gentle, because she's so little."

"I'll use a doll hairbrush," Alfie decided out loud. "What about a leash? Can Princess learn how to walk on a leash?"

"Nope. Never," Hanni said, shaking her head. "Because cats won't go anywhere unless they want to. And they hardly ever want to," she added. "They won't learn tricks, either," she informed Alfie. "Unless you get some really good treats. And even then, they have to be in the exact right mood."

"So what do kitties like to do?" Alfie asked, trying to picture Princess living in her room.

"Mostly play, when they're little," Hanni said, thinking about it. "And eat. And they sleep a *lot*. And sometimes they cuddle up and purr, and keep you company."

That last part sounded good, Alfie thought. Really good. She liked company, and her big brother was often too busy to play with her.

"Wanna do something?" she sometimes asked him.

"No way," EllRay would say. "Not unless you pay me."

"How much?"

"A nickel every five minutes," he'd say.

"Too much," Alfie would reply. "Anyway, you should pay me, EllRay. I'm more fun than you any day of the week."

"Huh?" EllRay might say, still only half listening.

He never really listened to her all the way, that was the thing. EllRay was always doing at least a couple of other things at the same time.

So if Princess was a good listener, that would be *great.*

"Okay," she told Hanni. "I think I'm good on kitties now."

"I'll give you a B+ in Kitten School," Hanni announced. "So let's go do something else for a change, okay?"

“We can work on our fairy garden again,” Alfie said. The girls had already begun creating a shady little world behind the Sobels’ fish pond. They’d made pathways and lined them with stones. They made a tiny table for the fairies, too.

“We can make the fairies a couple of little beds today,” Hanni suggested. “In case they get sleepy.”

“I’m putting ferns on mine,” Alfie said. “To make a really soft mattress.”

She should try that for Princess, too, she told herself, making a mental note.

“Me too,” Hanni said. “But I’m not copying you.”

“Go ahead and copy,” Alfie said, granting her permission.

“I already *said*, I’m not copying!” Hanni protested.

“Whatever you say,” Alfie told her, smiling as she shrugged.

Things felt a little more even now, anyway.

“So let’s go,” Hanni said, jumping to her feet.

“Bye, kitties,” Alfie called over her shoulder as they went out the laundry room door. “See ya later!”

A Kitty Palace

Alfie and Hanni were to be at the Jakeses' house the next day, Wednesday, and Alfie had a plan.

She was going to be in charge of this two-girl daycare club for once!

"We're gonna make a kitty palace for Princess," she told Hanni first thing, her brown eyes sparkling. "In my bedroom, okay? Only it's gotta be a secret."

Hanni and her parents had no idea that Alfie's mom and dad didn't know about Princess yet. And Alfie planned to keep it that way.

She had to have that kitty.

"How come it has to be a secret?" Hanni asked, curious.

"It'll be more fun that way," Alfie said. "C'mon,

let's go get some boxes from the garage. My dad said I could use as many as I want."

Alfie's father was a big saver-of-boxes, "just in case."

"You never know when a box will come in handy," he often said, stashing away another.

"It's for a building project," she had told him the night before.

He was thrilled. "Maybe you'll be an architect someday, Cricket," he said, beaming.

"This will be more like a sculpture, Dad," Alfie warned him. She didn't want him to get his hopes up too high—or ask to see the finished structure when it was done. He might be able to guess what it was for, and then where would she be?

Without a kitty, that's where.

Not to mention poor Princess's fate. The thought of someone else—a grouchy, no-fun old lady, or a noisy family with mean boys in it—adopting her kitten made Alfie's stomach hurt.

And her heart.

"So how are we going to stick these guys together?" Hanni asked in the garage as they stacked little boxes inside bigger ones.

"Duct tape," Alfie told her. "It works on anything, my dad says. Here, take a roll," she added, and each girl put a thick roll of duct tape on her wrist as if it were a giant silver bracelet. "I'm a fancy lady," Alfie said, admiring hers.

"No, *I'm* the fancy lady," Hanni said.

"Maybe we can both be fancy ladies," Alfie suggested.

"I guess," Hanni said. "But how is the kitty gonna climb up a bare cardboard tower?" she asked. "She's not magic, Alfie. She doesn't have sticky

feet. She's just a regular *kitten.* I mean, we have a cat tower for Domino at home, in our family room," she added, explaining. "Only it's made out of wood, and it's covered with carpet so she can scratch her claws on it and climb to the top. And feel superior to everyone."

Carpet?

Maybe a spare bath mat would do, Alfie thought, chewing her lip. Her mom would notice any missing chunks of regular carpet *for sure.*

"I'll take care of that later," she told Hanni, trying to sound more confident than she was feeling. "Princess will be able to climb this when we're done with it. My whole room is gonna be perfect for her," she added, pleased at the idea. "Perfect for a Princess."

"She'll fall and bang her furry little head," Hanni predicted, still wanting to be the expert.

"She won't," Alfie told her.

"But she could," Hanni said.

"But she won't. I'll watch her every second," Alfie promised. "Princess is talented," she tried to explain. "And really smart."

"You don't know that," Hanni said, laughing. "How can you tell?"

Hanni-the-Expert was kind of getting on her nerves, Alfie admitted silently.

"I just *can* tell," she said. "Are you gonna help me build, or not?"

"Sure, I'll help," Hanni said. "I don't care, as long as we get to do something fun after."

"Like make kitty toys," Alfie said, leading the way back into the house, her arms full of boxes. "I've got craft feathers and string and everything. We can invent some really cool toys, Hanni. And we can even make my new kitty a little crown out of gold paper and sparkle-stones," she added, picturing it.

"But do you have Ping-Pong balls?" Hanni asked, still wanting to be the boss of all kitten-related things.

"I can buy some," Alfie said as they headed up the stairs toward her room—only to be met by EllRay and his friend Marco as they came barreling down.

"Whoa," EllRay said, pausing. "You finally

moving out, Alf?" he asked, seeing the boxes. "It's about time!"

Marco laughed.

"Stop showing off," Alfie said, trying not to drop her boxes. "I'm not moving anywhere until I leave for San Francisco. *Alone.*"

"You're moving to San Francisco?" Hanni whispered, one step behind her.

"Not yet," Alfie whispered back. "We're making something," she told her brother. "Building something, really," she corrected herself.

"Building" sounded more important than "making."

"Building a dollhouse, probably," Marco piped up, staring at the two girls like he was on a field trip to a zoo.

This was a guy with no sisters, Alfie decided.

"Anyway, it's none of your business," she told EllRay, ignoring Marco. "So just go outside and play. And leave us alone."

"Well, scream if you get tangled up in that duct tape," EllRay said, laughing. "We'll come rescue you."

"That'll be the day," Alfie said over her shoulder as she finished climbing the stairs.

"And tell me when you're done building whatever-it-is," EllRay shouted after her. "Because Marco and me are the building inspectors."

"Yeah, right," Alfie called back. "You just stay out of my room!"

"'Maybe I will, and maybe I won't,'" EllRay teased, quoting her. He was already halfway out the door.

"You better stay out, that's all," Alfie said.

And she meant every word.

Operation Kittycat

It was Thursday, August seventeenth, Alfie told herself, looking at the calendar on the refrigerator door.

Eleven days since she'd first learned about the three weeks she would be spending with Hanni.

Eleven days until school started.

Floop.

That made today the belly-button of their two-girl daycare club experience.

Today would be spent at Hanni's house. And it was going to be major. Operation Kittycat was about to begin!

That meant there was an entire daycare club day to get through before Princess could come home with her, though. And Princess was all Alfie could think about.

Her kitty was the perfect purring handful of love, Alfie thought, feeling mushy, to her own surprise.

"Hi," Hanni said, greeting Alfie and her mom at the Sobels' front door. "Mom's on the phone in her office, but she says hi, too."

"Understood," Mrs. Jakes said, smiling. "It's a little cooler today, so you girls be sure to spend some of your time outside. This morning at least."

"Mom," Alfie protested. "We're supposed to 'organize our own activities in a fun but sensible way,' remember?"

Alfie had a strange knack for remembering what people said. EllRay told her this either made her the perfect witness for a trial or a real pain, depending.

"We're doing two things outdoors," Hanni told Alfie's mom. "My dad made this really cool ring toss game for the Fourth of July, and we're gonna play that on the lawn. And my mom invented a nature scavenger hunt for us, using our own backyard. And after that, we've got the wooden bead kit my auntie sent me. I'm gonna share with Alfie," she added—like it was nothing.

Ooh! Alfie had been eyeing that wooden bead kit all week. Her fingers itched to get going on a necklace or bracelet, maybe with a heart in the middle. She could wear it on the first day of school. So *that* was sweet.

Hanni really *was* a good sharer.

She might have to step up her own sharing game, Alfie admitted to herself.

But forget ring tosses, scavenger hunts, and even pretty bead necklaces. What Alfie wanted most was to get her hands on adorable little Princess once more. There were so many things to love about that small gray kitten!

Alfie liked hearing Princess practice her squeaky meow.

She loved it when Princess kicked at a toy mouse while gripping it with her tiny front paws.

And she liked to see Princess play with the shoelaces of the red sneakers sitting next to the laundry room door.

Just looking at Princess's pretty pink toe pads,

striped legs, white vest, and white whiskers made Alfie feel happy inside. Her new kitty was perfect.

And Princess was *something to love.*

"But remember," she told both Hanni and her own mom as they all stood in the Sobels' doorway. "I get to choose some of the stuff we do, too. That was the deal."

Maybe she could squeeze some Princess-time in there somewhere.

"You always want to do the same thing, though," Hanni said, laughing.

And—*boom.* Alfie knew that Hanni was about to spill the beans about the kittens.

About *Princess.*

Disaster!

"It's okay," she said quickly, to change the subject. "Your ideas sound good, Hanni. And it's really nice of you to share your beads."

"It certainly is," Alfie's mom said, getting ready to leave. "Now, Alfie, listen. Your brother will be picking you up this afternoon, okay? I have an appointment, so he'll be in charge until I get home."

Wait. *What?* This could ruin everything! Because EllRay was a big old snoop.

"I can walk home by myself, Mom," Alfie said, trying to sound calm.

"Out of the question."

"Or—or Hanni can walk me home," Alfie said, thinking fast.

"But then who would walk Hanni back home?" her mom asked, laughing. "We've got the makings of an old riddle here, Alfie. No, I think we'll stick with Plan A," she concluded, waving her hand in an airy way as she walked down the Sobels' brick path toward the sidewalk.

"EllRay could walk Hanni home!" Alfie shouted after her.

"But I don't want him to," Hanni whispered, tugging at Alfie's T-shirt. "I'm not used to big brothers, Alfie."

"Plan A," Alfie's mom repeated over her shoulder.

And she was gone.

10

Flat-Out Lying

"This is fun," Alfie said after lunch as the two girls worked on their bead necklaces in the cool of Hanni's bedroom—a very cute room, too, in Alfie's opinion. Hanni's bed was big and sat between two large windows, and her homework desk was built into a wall of shelves that held both books and toys. Hanni's desk chair was businesslike—but bright orange. Everything was very neat.

Where did she keep all her junk?

A round ottoman—as big across as a small trampoline—sat in the middle of Hanni's room. The wooden bead kit was on it, and Alfie and Hanni sat on the shiny wood floor as they worked.

"I'm gonna ask for one of these kits for my birthday in November," Alfie was saying as she

searched for a striped turquoise bead—barrel-shaped—to add to her necklace. Her color choices were casual, whatever looked good. Hanni had decided to invent a pattern, of course.

Purple—white—pink—white—pink—white—purple.

But both necklaces were looking good.

"Are you excited about starting school?" Alfie asked, poking the hard end of the pink necklace cord through her striped bead.

"Yeah. No. Kinda," Hanni admitted.

"Me too," Alfie said. "Only with me, it's more like *nervous*. I guess I wish we had a girl teacher, not a boy one."

Most of the teachers at Oak Glen Primary School were women, but Mr. Havens was definitely a man. A very large man. Alfie wondered suddenly if it ever bothered the boys, having girl teachers most of the time. She had never thought about it before.

"I know," Hanni said. "I'm scared he's gonna shout at us like he does on the playground, when he's coaching basketball."

"But EllRay says he's really nice, deep down inside," Alfie told her, trying to be fair.

"Yuck. Who cares what he's like inside?" Hanni asked, frowning as she searched for another round white bead. "If his outside is all yell-y and strict, second grade is gonna stink. Period."

"I bet the boys are happy he'll be our teacher," Alfie said, thinking about it.

"Maybe. But who cares if boys are happy or not?" Hanni asked, shaking her head and pursing her lips as she worked. "You only think of weird stuff like that because you have a brother, Alfie. I guess that kind of warps a girl."

"I guess," Alfie said. But she was glad she had a brother. "That reminds me," she said.

"Don't tell me," Hanni joked. "You want to go downstairs and visit the kitties again." She gave a comical sigh.

"Not really," Alfie said, fibbing. "But EllRay's picking me up later this afternoon, and I don't want him to know I'm bringing Princess home. He's the only one in my family who doesn't know about her, see," she added, the fib flying out of her mouth as easy as anything. "And I want it to be a surprise for everybody at the same time."

Okay, Alfie scolded herself. Now she was flat-out lying to Hanni, her brand-new friend. "Nice," as EllRay would say. And none of the Sobels knew she didn't have permission to bring Princess home.

But Princess needed her!

"We could find a kitten-sized box and decorate it," Hanni said, eager to take on another craft project. "We could even punch air holes in the top. You could tell EllRay it's just a pretty box to keep stuff in. He'll never guess what's inside. *Boys,*" she added with a snort meant to show how little they noticed things.

"I don't know," Alfie said, her forehead wrinkling as she thought. "Usually, punching air holes in a box is kind of a giveaway about what's inside."

"You could say it's a lizard," Hanni said.

"Then he'd want to see it for sure," Alfie told her.

"So we won't punch any air holes in the box," Hanni decided aloud. "Princess will be fine for just one block."

"But what if she meows?" Alfie asked.

"Talk real loud the whole time," Hanni advised her. "Or ask your brother to explain a video game or a movie plot or something. That's all boys talk about at school, isn't it? You'll be fine."

"If you say so," Alfie replied.

"Let's stop working on these necklaces and get started on that box," Hanni said, excited. "Because EllRay's gonna be here in *one hour.*"

"But can we finish the necklaces next week?" Alfie asked.

"Um-hmm," Hanni said, nodding. "Our last

week of the daycare club. My mom can show us how to do the clasps. Now help me put this stuff away," she said, back to her bossy old self. "And then I'll go ask Mom for a box for you-know-who."

"I hope this works," Alfie said, half under her breath. "The surprise, I mean. Don't say anything to give it away," she cautioned.

"Don't worry about it," Hanni told her. "I'm pretty good at keeping a secret when I have to."

Better than I am, probably, Alfie told herself, smiling—though she was keeping *this* secret, anyway. The one about Princess.

"What's so funny?" Hanni asked, putting each loose bead in its correct place in the box.

"Nothing," Alfie said. "I'm just happy, that's all."

Happy—and feeling guilty, she admitted silently. Because—*uh-oh.*

She was breaking a pretty big family rule.

Somehow, Operation Kittycat hadn't seemed real until this very moment!

But it was going to happen.

The question was, what would happen next?

11

Ready and Waiting

The hard part about pulling off Operation Kitty-cat was going to be leaving the Sobels' house fast enough, Alfie decided.

Before Mrs. Sobel said anything to EllRay about the kitten.

That's why she, Hanni, and Princess were waiting on the Sobels' front lawn when EllRay coasted up on his decal-decorated board.

"Hi! We did a craft project, too," Hanni told him, pointing first to EllRay's skateboard and then to the cardboard shoebox on the grass that held a snoozing Princess. Alfie and Hanni had decorated the box's sides with

press-on bows and fairy stickers. The box was tied shut with a piece of thick red yarn.

"What?" EllRay said, frowning. "This isn't some craft project, yo," he informed Hanni. "Skating is my *life*."

"What?" Hanni echoed, confused.

"Be quiet," Alfie told her brother. "Anyway, I thought *basketball* was your life. And Hanni was just trying to be nice. Not like some people around here."

"Yeah, nice," Hanni echoed. "Showing you this pretty box Alfie made to keep things in. Like—like seashells," she added, eager to come up with some fake but likely item. She wanted to help keep Princess a secret from EllRay—for now, anyway.

The box jiggled a little on the grass, and a bow fell off, but EllRay didn't notice. "Whatever," he said, shrugging. "It's okay, I guess. But it's not the same as my *board*. Now, c'mon, Alf," he said, impatient to get going. "You got everything? Because Mom said not to let you go waltzing off without all your stuff."

"I don't know *how* to waltz," Alfie told him, scooping up the box and cradling it to her chest.

"You know what I mean," he said.

"I got everything."

"Bye," Hanni told them, giving Alfie a special look that said, *Oh, boy! He is gonna be so surprised.* Hanni had no idea how surprised EllRay—and her parents—would be! It would be perfect, she thought, smiling. Because with Princess, it would be two against one at her house.

Two girls against one boy.

She could just see the look on EllRay's face. "No fair!" he would probably say.

"Life's not fair," she'd tell him. "That's what Mom always says. That, and 'It's not a contest.'"

"That doesn't make it right," EllRay would grumble.

"Maybe it does, and maybe it doesn't," she'd say, smiling. "But I win."

Score!

But EllRay would not be surprised for a while, Alfie vowed on Hanni's front lawn, trying to cross her fingers and hold the kitten box at the same time.

"You didn't have to be so mean to Hanni," Alfie told EllRay as they walked home.

"I wasn't mean," he said, barcly listening as he rolled along on his board, going as slowly as possible. "I was telling her the truth, that's all. And she'd better learn not to make fun of sixth-graders, too. So I was really doing her a favor."

"She wasn't making fun," Alfie said, feeling Princess thump around inside the box. "She was chatting, that's all."

"Well, you don't know how to *waltz*, and I don't know how to *chat*," EllRay said.

"Huh! You can say that again," Alfie told him. "Only don't."

"Don't what?"

"Don't say that again. Just—just skate on home," Alfie told him. "I'll be right behind you."

"I can't leave you standing here," EllRay said. "It would be just my luck if you got lost or something. I'd never hear the end of it."

"I can see the house!" Alfie exclaimed. "How could I get lost?"

Princess was really kicking up her heels—two heels? four heels?—inside the box by now, but EllRay didn't notice.

"Just stop talking," he said. "I'm in charge, remember. And what I say goes."

"Yeah. It goes in one ear and out the other," Alfie told him, repeating an old saying she'd once heard.

Zing.

"I wouldn't brag about that," EllRay said, turning up the driveway. "Because it means there's nothing inside your head. So, *ha*."

"*Ha* back at you," Alfie said.

"Do I have to tell you to go to your room?" EllRay half teased as he unlocked the kitchen door.

"Go ahead and try," Alfie said, unable to believe her luck. "I dare you."

And she had thought she would have to find

some excuse not to hang out with him, but here he was—just handing it to her. *Score.*

Her bedroom was ready and waiting for Princess, its tiny new occupant.

Operation Kittycat was almost complete!

"Okay," EllRay said, taking the dare. "*Go to your room.* But grab a banana or something first," he added, clearly wanting to back down. "Because they'll yell at me if you starve."

"No," Alfie called out, heading toward the stairs. "I'm too busy obeying your royal orders, *EllRay.* I don't have time for mere food."

"Okay," EllRay yelled after her. "See if I care. This is the last time I try and do something nice for *you.*"

"Like sending me to my room?" Alfie shouted from the upstairs hall—having the last word.

And that was one of her favorite things in the world to do.

"We're home," she whispered to Princess, and she opened her bedroom door.

Dinner in a Haunted House

"Don't forget the salad," Mrs. Jakes told Alfie and EllRay at dinner that night. "And not just two or three pieces of lettuce for decoration, either," she added. "I know your little ways."

Salad would be fine, Alfie thought, if it wasn't for all the weird stuff her mother put in it.

Beans and nuts.

Raw and cooked vegetables.

Sometimes pieces of fruit.

Alfie liked most of these things on their own, but she did not like them to surprise her by sneaking into other food.

Eek!

And her mom bought so many different kinds of lettuce at the farmers' market that Alfie was pretty sure there had to be a curly green weed or two in there somewhere.

Maybe even a bug.

"Perhaps we should begin dinner with our salad from now on," Alfie's dad said, his forehead wrinkling as he thought about it. "That way, it would be sure to be eaten."

Her scientist-professor father was tall and thin. He wore glasses and kept his hair cut very short. He was always coming up with sensible suggestions like the one about eating salad first, Alfie thought, hiding a sigh. She rearranged the salad on her plate to make her portion look bigger.

Piece of chicken, biscuit, peas, and now—*salad.*

She glanced up at the ceiling, wondering what Princess was doing.

Enjoying her kitten chow dinner?

Lapping up water with her naturally curly tongue?

Climbing the curtains again? Because that was what she had been doing ever since they got home, Alfie reminded herself, frowning.

Princess showed no interest at all in the cardboard cat tower, no matter how many treats Alfie hid in its corners. Instead, the kitten headed straight for the curtains above Alfie's desk. Then, using her tiny but very sharp claws, she pulled herself up them—like a small, gray King Kong climbing the Empire State Building.

Then the kitty just *hung* there—like some weird Christmas ornament.

She was always right out of Alfie's reach, too,

unless Alfie cleared off her desk and climbed up on it to unhook the wiggly gray kitty from the sagging fabric.

Then Princess did it again and again until dinner was ready.

Yeesh!

This had not been the cuddly afternoon Alfie imagined it would be.

And her mom was *definitely* going to notice shredded curtains if Princess kept this up, Alfie thought, peeking up at the ceiling again.

"What are you staring at?" EllRay asked from across the table. "Is there a spider up there?"

"There had better not be a spider, or it's going to see some action from your mother," Mr. Jakes said from the end of the table. He laughed as he cut his piece of chicken.

"If anything, it's a fly," Mrs. Jakes said. "Which, by the way, is what happens when you leave the back door open in the summer, *children*."

"Not to mention losing all that nice cold bought air," her husband added.

"Bought air" is what Mr. Jakes called house air that had been either air-conditioned or, in the winter, heated. "At great expense to the management," he sometimes added.

"The management" was her mom and dad, Alfie knew from past experierience. He was talking about the gas and electric bills.

"I didn't leave the door open," EllRay said automatically.

"Me neither," Alfie chimed in.

And that was when they heard the muffled crash—from Alfie's room, of course.

Princess.

The kitten had probably knocked over the failed cat tower or pulled off some other amazing acrobatic feat. Or maybe the curtains had fallen down!

"I didn't hear anything," Alfie said, way too fast.

"I did. What was it?" Alfie's mom asked, on her feet in a flash. "Is somebody in the house? Warren, you'd better go take a look."

"No! It was me," Alfie said before her dad could dash upstairs with a baseball bat—and discover her furry purry secret.

Because then Operation Kittycat would be over for good.

Finished.

"Done-zo," as EllRay sometimes said.

And she needed time, Alfie reminded herself—time to be able to show her mom and dad that she was not allergic to animal fur. This was what would allow her to prove her case.

"Yeah," EllRay said, laughing a little. "It was you, because you can be two places at the same time. Right? You're just that amazing."

"No," Alfie said, trying to match his sarcasm. "It's because I think I left my daycamp stuff on the edge of my bed. Either that, or it's because my library books fell over. That's probably what happened, because I had them stacked crooked on the desk chair," she added as her mother settled back into her seat.

But Mrs. Jakes was still listening—*hard.*

And Alfie crossed her fingers under the table, hoping like anything that Princess would settle down.

Please, please, please, she thought.

"Yo," EllRay said after swallowing a mouthful of honey-smeared biscuit. "It's like having dinner in a haunted house around here."

“Don’t say ‘yo’ at the table, sweetie,” his mother reminded him.

“Okay,” EllRay said. “But I read this book once about haunted houses,” he went on. “And if it gets really cold in here all of a sudden, or if the lights go off *and* there are more weird noises, we should probably do something about it.”

"Right. Like get our heads examined," his father—Dr. Jakes the scientist—said, grimacing. "Haunted houses," he added with a laugh. "What next? And our lights aren't even *on,* son, so they can hardly go off," he pointed out. "It's August. If anyone has left any lights blazing away in this house during daylight hours, they're going to hear about it from your mother and me. Eat your salad, Cricket," he added, noticing Alfie's plate.

And Alfie was so eager to keep dinner humming along smoothly—with no more talk about haunted house noises—that she finished every single bite of salad on her plate.

Even the mysterious parts.

Family Rules

"Oh, no," Alfie groaned.

It was the next morning, Saturday. She wanted to stay home with Princess—but she had to go to the farmers' market with her mom. It was their weekend ritual, and there was no getting out of it, Alfie knew. Asking to stay home would just make her mother suspicious.

And EllRay and their dad had already left for their morning together, so they couldn't babysit her.

But a speedy ninety minutes later, Alfie was back from the market.

She had not lingered near the best free samples.

Or begged her mom to buy homemade cinnamon rolls from the bread lady.

Or watched the little kids dance in front of the

drummer, secretly wishing she could join in.

And once Alfie had helped her mother carry in the canvas totes and net bags full of plump strawberries, silky-topped ears of corn, tomatoes, clusters of the too-hot radishes her dad loved, and the weird lettuces that would lurk in future salads, she was free to go upstairs to her room.

To Princess.

"I'm home, kitty," Alfie announced, opening her bedroom door with caution. She squeezed into the room. At once, the sweet fragrance of strawberries lingering in her nostrils fought with the stink of the litter box.

Ew!

No Princess. Where was she this time?

Disguised among the stuffed animals lined up at the head of Alfie's bed? Smooshed in behind her pillows?

Curled up among the clothes in the hamper?

In the two days Princess had been living at the Jakeses' house, Alfie had found her sleeping in all three places—when she wasn't hanging from the curtains.

"Here, kitty-kitty-kitty," Alfie called out in a tempting way.

"Mew," came the rusty-sounding reply from her bookcase.

"Oh, Princess-kitty," Alfie crooned, hurrying over. "How did you climb up there? You little silly." She plucked Princess from the bookshelf and held her tight against her chest. She tried to remember the way she felt the first time she had held her kitten—the Tuesday before last. Only eleven days ago!

How had her life gotten so complicated in just eleven days?

She hadn't known much about kittens then, Alfie admitted now—except that she wanted one. And now she was wearing jeans instead of comfy summer shorts because of the tiny scratches that decorated her legs. Princess had taken to climbing up Alfie's jammie bottoms as if Alfie herself were the cat tower in this house.

Her mom would be sure to ask questions if she saw those scratches.

Also, the litter box in the corner was pretty

smelly, Alfie admitted silently. And all because of one tiny kitten! Who would have guessed? Her mom was sure to notice before long.

She would have to sneak another bag of gritty little poos downstairs again and hide it in the trash, Alfie told herself, shuddering.

Yuck on top of *yuck*.

The box needed more litter, too, in Alfie's opinion. She had only been able to bring home a couple of small bags of it from the Sobels' house.

Her fourteen dollars wouldn't last long the way things were going, she thought gloomily.

But there were some excellent things about having a kitten in the house, Alfie reminded herself as she curled up on the bed with her treasure, her prize, her furry Princess. Operation Kittycat had been a success! She wasn't sniffling or sneezing, for one thing—and that proved she was right about not being allergic to cats.

And Alfie loved being right.

But better than that was the cozy feeling she had whenever she snuggled with Princess—who definitely was *not* homesick, Alfie assured herself, in spite of the gray kitten's lonely-sounding *mews*.

Well, being *a little* lonely was natural, she thought, reconsidering. Even she, Alfie, had been kind of homesick a couple of times last year in first grade. And at Little Acorns Daycamp this summer—and that wasn't even a sleep-away camp.

Princess was fun, too. That was another good thing. She loved chasing the end of a feather from

Alfie's craft supplies as Alfie dragged it back and forth across her bedspread.

Also, Princess purred like anything when Alfie petted her.

And this kitten really *was* a good listener.

"Here's the thing, Princess," Alfie murmured, running a finger down her kitty's silky white vest. "Our family has these rules, see. Only some of them don't make very much sense. But you're supposed to follow them anyway."

Family rules like *"No Snacking Before Dinner,"* because supposedly that might make you ruin your appetite. But neither she nor EllRay *ever* had a problem with ruined appetites, Alfie reminded herself now. Not even at a picnic, where potato chips and dip, hard-boiled eggs, and even spicy chicken wings might be devoured before the main part of the meal.

Family rules like *"Don't Ask for Stuff in the Supermarket."* But what if you were just reminding your mom or dad to buy something—like bread? That was asking, wasn't it?

This would be a good example to use when she

got in trouble for breaking the family rule about pets, Alfie told herself. And that was sure to be pretty soon, she realized, frowning.

She petted Princess a little faster.

Some family rules just made sense, of course—rules like *"No Swearing,"* and *"No Spitting or Hitting." Duh.* You almost didn't even have to say them. And Alfie was absolutely counting on the *"Knock Before Entering"* rule to help her keep Princess a secret as long as possible.

Her *Privacy, Please!* doorknob sign was shedding glitter this very moment.

But what about the rule *"Clean Up Your Mess"*? Look at her mom's writing desk! Its edges were covered with stacks of papers, either loose or clipped together. Looking at that desk was like staring at a year's worth of homework jammed into a primary school cubby, Alfie told herself now. Books were piled into small towers on the floor next to her mom's desk, too.

Alfie wasn't allowed to leave stuff lying around this way.

So that family rule really meant *"Clean Up Your*

Mess" when her mom was saying it, Alfie thought, getting ready for the argument that was sure to come.

But—she had just plain broken a rule, after all. There was no denying it!

And she was going to have to come clean about it sooner or later.

"Make that later," Alfie whispered, shoving aside her small, hard lump of guilt for the moment, flopping back on her bed and lifting Princess high in the air. Princess looked like a furry gray starfish if you squinted your eyes, Alfie thought, delighted.

She loved Princess.

And that had to count for something, didn't it?

Take Your Medicine

"Your room or my room?" EllRay asked Alfie the next night, Sunday. Board game night.

"Your room," Alfie said quickly—because her room had been taken over by one small kitten. Abandoned cardboard boxes meant for the cat tower lay tumbled in the corner. She had moved Princess's litter box from under her bed to the closet. But now it was stinking up her clothes, even the new things her mom had bought for second grade.

And Alfie did *not* want to become known as "the girl with the poopy-smelling clothes" when school started. That was not a mark she wanted to have on her imaginary second grade whiteboard.

Alfie's curtains sagged, but Princess never

tired of climbing them—and then hanging like a bat, just out of reach.

It was as if vandals had taken over her once-pretty room, Alfie thought. All that was missing was graffiti on the walls.

"Your room," Alfie said again.

"I heard you the first time," her brother told her, leading the way up the stairs. "Want to play that mystery game?"

"Nuh-uh. It kinda gives me nightmares," Alfie admitted.

"It's not *real*," EllRay scoffed. "It's just little cartoon guys who are the crime victims."

"Nightmares aren't real either," Alfie pointed out. "I mean, they're not real things you can touch. But they're still scary. Let's play that game where you drop the discs until you get a bunch of them in a row. Only I get to be red this time. What's for snack?" she asked as EllRay rummaged in his closet for the game.

"Fruit pieces and some weird kind of dip," her brother told her. "Mom found a recipe. She's bringing it up in a minute."

Alfie padded over to his bedroom door and

opened it wider, so their mother would know for sure what room they were in. Her furry purry secret was going to be discovered before long, she now knew—but not tonight.

Please not tonight, Alfie thought, because she still didn't know how she was going to explain Operation Kittycat—and her absolute *need* for a kitten to love—to her mom and dad.

❊ ❊ ❊

Half an hour later, she and EllRay were well into their third game. Their fingers were sticky from the fluffy white dip their mom had brought upstairs with cut-up strawberries, bananas, and a pile of paper towels.

And then—

Bam!

The crash came from next-door.

From Alfie's room.

EllRay jumped. "There's that ghost again," he said, laughing.

But only a little.

"I didn't hear anything," Alfie said, inspecting

one of her red plastic discs as if it might suddenly have changed color.

"You keep saying that," her brother told her. "Whenever there's a funny noise."

"There wasn't a funny noise," Alfie quickly insisted. "And anyway, it wasn't very loud."

EllRay shot her a look. "Okay, listen," he said, his voice flat. "What"s going on?"

"Nothing," Alfie said. "Except—"

Was she really about to say this?

"Except—*something,*" she told her brother.

Because why not spread the news—and the guilt—around a little? It might make her feel a little better about the whole rule-breaking thing, Alfie told herself.

"Something like what?" EllRay said. "What are you up to, Alf?"

"Do you really want to know?" Alfie asked, her eyes beginning to sparkle.

"Not if it's gonna get me in trouble," EllRay said, clapping his hands over his ears.

"Quit it," Alfie said, tugging at one of his arms. "I know you can still hear me, EllRay."

"Okay. Spit it out, then," EllRay said. "What's

going on in your room? What do you have hidden in there?"

Alfie took a deep, shaky breath. "Close your eyes and I'll go get her," she said.

"*Her?*" EllRay exclaimed. "There's a *girl* in your room?"

"Shh," Alfie said, finger to her lips. "Maybe there is, and maybe there isn't. Go on, EllRay. Close your eyes."

When her brother finally did as she asked, Alfie darted off—but was back in a moment with a squirming Princess held tight against her chest.

"Now open your eyes," Alfie told her brother.

EllRay did, then he blinked a couple of times. "*Yeesh,*" he said quietly, seeing the gray-and-white kitten for the first time.

"But *yeesh* in a good way, right?" Alfie said, her heart pounding. "Don't you just love her? Don't you want to hold her?" she asked, trying to hand Princess to him in what she hoped was a tempting way. "Isn't she cute?"

"All kittens are cute," EllRay said. "That's their business, being cute. But do Mom and Dad know anything about this?" His arms remained folded tightly against his chest as if he were determined not to touch this kitten even once.

Alfie guessed he didn't want any kitty-guilt rubbing off on him.

"No-o-o," she admitted slowly. "And you're not gonna tell them, either."

"Because you are," he informed her.

"Yeah. Someday, I guess," Alfie agreed. "Maybe after school starts?" She made it a question.

"That's not for another whole week," EllRay reminded her. "How long has that cat been living here?"

"Kind of like three days," Alfie said. "This will be her fourth night. Her name is Princess, by the way. *Kitty-kitty-kitty,*" she added, rubbing noses with the kitten.

EllRay's eyes narrowed. "That girl Hanni's behind all this, isn't she?" he said, like it was a fact. "She probably bossed you into sneaking this kitten home with you."

"For *free,*" Alfie pointed out, hoping this would help her score a few points. "And Hanni doesn't know I didn't have permission. I didn't want to sound *lame,* like we're some weird family that doesn't like pets. And—I just really needed a kitten, that's all."

Her voice broke, saying these last words.

EllRay shook his head. "Nobody 'needs a kitten,'" he informed his little sister. "Kittens aren't like food. They're not like air. They're not like water."

"I needed one," Alfie insisted.

"Well, you're gonna have to go tell Mom and Dad about it," he announced.

"What, *now*?" Alfie asked.

"Yeah," he said. "You already waited too long. It's not gonna get any better the longer you wait. Just go downstairs and get it over with," he advised.

"I know! I'll bring Princess with me," Alfie said, inspired. Who could resist a kitten?

"Nope. Bad idea," EllRay said. "Believe me on this one, Alf. Look, I'll babysit it for you while you go downstairs and confess."

"*Princess,*" Alfie murmured. "She's a girl, not an 'it,' and her name is Princess, EllRay. You can at least say her name."

"Okay. *Princess,*" EllRay said. "Hand her over and get going."

"Really?" Alfie asked, her voice small. "All by myself?"

"Really," EllRay said, but then his voice softened, seeing the look on her face. "Just tell them what you did and why you did it, Alfie," he suggested. "And then go ahead and take the consequences. You gotta come clean."

That basically meant "confess and take your punishment," Alfie knew.

Only she didn't want any punishment. Who did? Ever?

She just wanted Princess!

"Go on," EllRay said, impatient now.

But there was sympathy in his eyes.

"All right. I'm *going*," Alfie told him. "Only don't let them take her away, no matter how mad they get. Okay? Promise?"

"Just go," EllRay said.

Coming Clean

"Excuse me. Hi," Alfie said, feeling awkward as she drifted into the family room a few minutes later. This was after the world's slowest walk downstairs.

Her heart was pounding.

Her parents didn't even have the TV on, she noticed, surprised. Instead, they were each stretched out on the sectional, reading. And the strange thought suddenly occurred to Alfie that maybe Sunday night was special for them, too.

"What's up, Cricket?" her dad asked, lowering the book he was reading. "Trouble in game-land?"

"Not exactly," Alfie said, perching on a nearby chair. It was as if she were visiting strangers.

What had she been *thinking,* bringing Princess

home without permission like that?

Well, she'd been thinking that Operation Kittycat would make it easier for her to start a new school year with a maybe-scary new teacher, that's what, Alfie told herself.

With a cute new mark on an almost-clean whiteboard.

It would be easier to meet new kids in class if she had something to talk about, for once.

And it would be easier on the days that things went wrong, too—because with a kitty, she would have something good to come home to. Something to cuddle and talk with. Something to take care of. Something to love.

Of course, things hadn't exactly worked out the way she had imagined, Alfie confessed to herself.

For example, her closet now smelled. *Bad.*

And her room was "a shambles," as her mother would say.

And her desk—brand-new school supplies arranged *just so*—was a mess, thanks to Princess's curtain acrobatics, and her wild ways in general.

Princess was more whirlwind than kitten, it seemed.

Yet she, Alfie Jakes, was truly in love with that crazy kitten. What if she had to give her kitty back to the Sobels?

She *needed* Princess, and Princess needed her.

"'Not exactly?'" her mother echoed. "Then what *is* it, exactly?" she asked, setting down her book with obvious reluctance.

"I—I made a little mistake," Alfie managed to say, but then she stopped. Sneaking Princess home hadn't really been a *mistake,* she reminded herself. That is, it had been wrong, so it was a mistake in that way. But she'd done it on purpose.

And it was a big mistake, not a little one.

The thing was, though, breaking this family rule had seemed worth getting into any amount of trouble for—when she did it.

But now she had to pay the price.

"Can you be a bit more clear?" Alfie's dad asked, sitting up straighter on the sofa and planting his feet on the floor.

Uh-oh, Alfie thought, her heat pounding even harder than before. But she had better get it over with, like EllRay said. "We have a kitten," she

announced, staring down at the floor.

A brief but electric silence seemed to fill the family room. "You mean you *want* a kitten," Alfie's mom finally said. "And you'd like to talk about that, even though you know the reason against it."

"Which isn't even true," Alfie blurted out before she could stop herself.

"What part of it isn't true?" her mom asked, frowning.

"The whole thing. The being-allergic part," Alfie said. "Because I'm not, and I can prove it. We've had a kitty living in this house for three whole days! And look, no runny nose. I call her Princess," she added, as if this excellent name might be the random detail that would win over her gaping parents.

Mrs. Jakes looked confused. "Do you mean like a pretend kitty?" she asked. "Because the '*No Pets*' rule doesn't apply to imaginary animals, sweetie."

And of course Alfie jumped right in. "But what if one of our family rules is a *bad* rule?" she asked, daring to look her mom in the eye for the first time since coming downstairs. "What if it doesn't make any sense, and it's just plain *wrong*?"

"Then we talk about changing it," Alfie's father said in his deepest, most rumbly voice. "We have a family meeting and discuss it. We mull it over. We *think* about it."

"Forever and ever," Alfie said. "Only there wasn't time, Dad. Because if I didn't bring Princess home, the wrong person would have taken her. A mean person, maybe. Or a *criminal.*"

"Warren," Alfie's mother said. "I think she's talking about a real cat."

"A *kitten,*" Alfie corrected her. "A baby, Mom. A helpless little baby."

"Where did you get it?" her dad asked, but Alfie didn't answer. She wanted to keep the Sobels out of this, especially her new friend Hanni.

"It had to be from Hanni's house," Mom-the-Mind-Reader said, thinking about it. "That's the only place Alfie has been recently."

"But this wasn't Hanni's fault," Alfie was quick to say. "She didn't know I didn't have permission to bring Princess home. The Sobels didn't know about the rule."

"Wait a minute," her dad said, holding his hand up in the air. "You're really telling us that you decided to pick and choose among our family rules, Alfie? All on your own, without any discussion? As if you were at some restaurant buffet, and you could simply select the rules you liked and ignore the ones you didn't?"

Tears were pricking at Alfie's eyes. Her dad sounded really mad at her! And for a goofy reason, too. He was talking about how wrong she was about the rules, not how right she was about the kitten. "I wouldn't exactly put it *that* way," she began in a wobbly voice.

"I'll bet you wouldn't," her father said.

By now, Alfie was just trying not to cry. Tears were not going to save Princess.

"Where is this cat?" Alfie's mother asked.

"Kitten," Alfie corrected her, and then wished she hadn't. "She's upstairs with EllRay. And she's had her shots and everything. I *need* her, Mom."

"EllRay knew about this?" Mr. Jakes asked.

"No!" Alfie said, frantic to keep her big brother out of trouble. "He *didn't* know, I promise. I only told him tonight because I had to."

"And just where has the kitten been living all this time?" her mother asked.

"In my bedroom."

"The one with the *Privacy, Please!* sign on the door?" her mom asked in an icy voice. "The room I allowed you to keep private all summer because you promised you could keep it clean without me checking on it all the time? That bedroom?"

"Uh-huh," Alfie mumbled, nodding as she stared at the floor.

One hot tear was now making its way down her cheek, but she was determined to hide it.

"Well, obviously we'll have to take another look at *that* decision," her mother said, getting to her feet and heading toward the hall. "But for now, I'm going upstairs to take a look at just how bad this situation really is."

"No, wait," Alfie cried, springing across the room like the cricket she used to be. "I'll go with you!"

"Come back here at once, Alfleta Jakes," her father said. "You will sit in that chair until your mother comes downstairs with her report."

"But—"

"Sit."

"Yes, sir."

16

What in the World Were You Thinking?

The next morning, Monday, Alfie woke early—and all alone. Her head ached, and her face felt tight from the tears she'd shed in private the night before.

"Oh, Princess," she whispered.

But there was no Princess curled up next to her. Alfie petted the empty spot on her blanket anyway, imagining the kitten's answering purr.

Alfie's mom and dad had not yet decided what to do about "the situation," as they were calling it. But they'd agreed Princess was not to sleep in Alfie's room.

So the kitten had spent the night somewhere else in the house—and climbed someone else's curtains.

Alfie's room looked different now. The empty cardboard boxes were back in the garage, folded, stacked, and awaiting their next adventure. The sagging, claw-pulled curtains above her desk had been straightened. The litter box—one of her mother's extra baking dishes—had disappeared, too, straight into the trash, Alfie was told.

"For heaven's sake," her mother had said, shaking her head in disgust.

Princess's handmade toys were gone as well, and the *Privacy, Please!* sign removed from Alfie's door. "You earn that kind of privilege," Alfie's parents had reminded her the night before. "And you can lose it, too, when you pull a sneaky stunt like that."

"Maybe it was too much privacy too soon," her mom had remarked, taking some of the blame for herself. But that only made Alfie feel worse.

Her mom and dad had tucked her in last night, though—and kissed her good night the same as always, Alfie reminded herself in the early morning light. Yes, there would be what her parents called "consequences." But they still loved her.

EllRay felt okay about her, too, and Alfie knew it.

After her parents had said good night, he knocked three times on the wall that separated their rooms. That was their secret signal for *Hi, I'm here.*

I am too, she knocked back.

But this morning was the start of the last week of the two-girl daycare club. Alfie would be spending today at Hanni's house, because Mrs. Jakes had a dentist appointment.

Alfie just hoped Hanni didn't ask how things had gone last night.

And she hoped Princess would still be there when she got home.

Oh, Princess!

"Early morning breakfast meeting," her mom said, poking her head into Alfie's room. "In the kitchen, in half an hour. Bed made, and please be dressed and ready to leave for Hanni's house right after. Get a wiggle on, Miss Alfie."

"Okay," Alfie said, reluctant to leave the peaceful cocoon of her bed.

But she had better "get it over with," as EllRay would say. Her mom and dad must have made their decision about Princess, and she might as well hear it.

Mr. Jakes was looking sharp as he sipped his coffee, ready for a day of meetings, research, or whatever it was he did at his San Diego college before fall classes began. "Take a seat and pour your cereal, Alfie," he said when she walked into the kitchen.

No more "Cricket," Alfie guessed. Maybe ever again.

"I don't think I can eat anything," she said, hoping this might let her dad know how sad and sorry she was about tricking them.

Okay, *lying* to them, basically—even if she had never actually said, *"I did not bring a kitten home from Hanni's house!*

"And her name is not Princess!

"And she's not living in my room and tearing it apart!"

"Good, we're all here," Alfie's mom said, coming into the kitchen.

EllRay was probably hiding out in his room, Alfie thought. But that was what she would be doing, if he was the one called to the "early morning breakfast meeting."

Alfie poured herself a heaping bowl of the

healthiest cereal they had, hoping that might score her a few points. All she wanted was to ask, "Can we keep Princess?" but she knew that question would backfire.

So she waited.

"Before we begin," her dad asked his daughter, "what in the world were you thinking?"

"I *wasn't* thinking. Not at first," Alfie admitted. "I was *wanting.* Hanni's kitties took me by surprise, see," she tried to explain. "And I just—I just wanted one. I knew I wasn't really allergic, because I've played with friends' cats before. But then the whole thing jumped from wanting to *needing.*"

"'Needing,'" her mother echoed.

"Explain, please," her father said, sounding very professor-like.

"See, school is about to start, right?" Alfie began. "In just one more week. A whole new grade, with new kids to meet, and a new teacher, too. Mr. Havens. EllRay says he's strict, too, and I wanted to get off to a really good start," she continued. "I just kind of figured that having a kitty at home might make everything easier to take."

"How's that?" her mother asked. "You've never

had any trouble making friends, Alfie."

"But when I came home after school, the kitty would be glad to see me," Alfie tried to explain. "I could talk to her about stuff, no matter what happened during the day. Good or bad."

"*I'm* glad to see you when you get home," her mom protested. "I talk to you, Alfie."

"But you don't need me to take care of you," Alfie said. "A kitty would."

"And who did you think would be taking care of the kitten during the day, when you're in school?" her father asked. "Did you really think your mother needed something else to do five days a week? An additional chore?"

Huh? "I guess I wasn't thinking about Mom," Alfie admitted. "But cats mostly sleep, Hanni says."

"Cats do, maybe," Alfie's father said. "Kittens definitely don't."

So that solved the mystery of where Princess had spent the night.

Such a Mess-Up

Alfie's dad cleared his throat. "There are three issues we need to discuss," he began, and Alfie could feel her heart go down, down, down in her chest like a very small elevator.

Three issues? Not just one?

"First," Mr. Jakes said, "you broke a family rule, Alfie. Now, I understand that you think that rule is wrong. But when a rule is wrong, you get to work changing it. You don't simply ignore it and do whatever you please."

"Yes, sir," Alfie replied.

"Second," her father said after exchanging a look with his wife, "you deceived your mother and me for three entire days." He looked—*disappointed* in her, Alfie saw.

Cringe.

"I'm not arguing, but what does 'deceived' mean?" she asked quietly.

"It means you misled us on purpose in order to get your own way," her mom told her, stirring honey into her tea as if this were an ordinary thing to say.

"Oh," Alfie said. "I guess I did that."

"You *did* do that," her father corrected her. "And third, there's the cat situation. What are we going to do about the cat?"

"And what about Alfie's consequences?" Mrs. Jakes asked, piling on.

"I have an idea," Alfie said, speaking up in spite of the lonely spot in her chest where her heart used to be. "I think we should decide that I already learned my lesson! And that we should keep the kitty. Keep Princess."

It was worth a try.

"Your mother and I had some other ideas," Alfie's father said.

"First," Alfie's mom said, "I want you to promise to talk to us about the family rules if you have a problem with one of them. I'm not saying we will

change that rule, but we'll certainly consider it if you or EllRay make a good enough case."

"Okay," Alfie mumbled. She guessed she could do that.

"Meanwhile," her dad said as if he and his wife were a team and Mrs. Jakes had just passed him the ball, "you'll pay us back for the baking dish and spoon we need to replace. They were our property, so it's only fair. And if you don't have enough money in your ballerina jewelry box, we'll take a little out of your allowance each week."

"Okay," Alfie said. But—*ouch.*

"In addition to that," her mom said, "because of the deception, there will be no TV or video games for you for an entire week, Miss Alfie. Also, you will apologize to each of us."

"Can I do that part now?" Alfie asked, because she really wanted to. She *hated* the guilty feeling she'd had in her tummy for more than a week. Her mom always said that the guilt a person felt was an early warning device. It was that person's way of telling themselves they were doing something wrong, and to just *quit* it. So that feeling was a gift, Mom said.

And now Alfie knew she was right.

"I apologize," she said, meaning it. "I shouldn't have tried to trick you guys that way. Or any way," she added before her dad could correct her. "I was wrong."

"We accept your apology," her father said, reaching out to shake her hand. Her mom shook

Alfie's hand too, and Alfie felt as though she'd just stepped out of a warm shower, she felt so sweet and clean.

"But—what about Princess?" she finally dared ask. "It's not *her* fault I was such a mess-up. And I don't want her to be an orphan at the animal shelter."

"I called Mrs. Sobel last night," Alfie's mother said, "and I told her the whole story."

Oh, no, Alfie thought, her eyes wide. Would busy, modern, tidy, lemony Mrs. Sobel dislike her now—and tell Hanni to stay away from her, no matter what?

Was loneliness going to be Alfie's souvenir from the two-girl daycare club? That, and a big scribble-scrabble mess on her imaginary second grade whiteboard?

"And Hanni's mom said she would take the kitten back, if that's what we wanted," Alfie's mother continued. "She was very understanding about the whole thing. She even apologized to *me*, which really went above and beyond."

Oh, Alfie thought, stunned.

So that was that. The worst had happened.

No more Princess.

Nobody to take care of.

Nothing little to love.

Alfie tried to remember how to breathe.

"Your mother told Mrs. Sobel thank you, but we've decided to keep the cat," Alfie's dad said, seeing the look on his daughter's face. "She's a cutie, and if no one's allergic to her—"

"We're not," Alfie said, hardly able to believe her luck.

Princess!

"But she will be a family pet," her mother was quick to say. "Not just yours, young lady—even though you'll be the only one doing litter box duty for a while."

"Until October first," Alfie's dad announced, as if he'd already written it on the refrigerator calendar. "After that, you and EllRay will take turns."

"EllRay likes her, too?" Alfie asked.

"He's crazy about her," Mr. Jakes said, getting to his feet. "And now, let's draw a line through this whole episode and get on with the rest of our lives."

Thank goodness, Alfie thought. "I really am sorry," she told her parents again.

"We know, Cricket," her father said, reeling her in for a big daddy-hug before heading for work.

Cricket!

"We know," her mother echoed, smiling. "You're our good girl. But you and I are going to have to scoot so we don't keep Hanni waiting—*or* the dentist."

"Okay," Alfie said. "I'll go get my stuff. Can I say good-bye to Princess, though?"

"I suppose," her mom said. "She's in our bathroom. Just keep the toilet lid down so she doesn't fall in."

"Okay," Alfie said again. "And—thanks, Mom," she added softly.

"You're welcome, sweetie."

A Jakes Family Portrait

"Hi," Alfie said ten minutes later when the Sobels' front door opened. Hanni and Mrs. Sobel had both come to the door today.

Seeing Mrs. Sobel, Alfie felt her face grow warm. "Mom just dropped me off. She had to hurry to her dentist appointment," she told Mrs. Sobel while scuffing the doormat with the toe of her pink sandal. She hoped she wasn't about to hear another lecture about how naughty she'd been. In front of Hanni, too!

If she—Alfie—didn't already know that, who did?

But Mrs. Sobel didn't say a word about Princess. "It's going to be a hot one again," she said instead, leading the girls into the house. "So if you're planning any outdoor adventures, better get started early."

"We're gonna play near the pond," Hanni told her mom. "It's nice out there. *C'mon,*" she whispered to Alfie when her mom had disappeared into her office. "You have to tell me everything that happened."

And Hanni led the way outside, down the patio steps and across a stretch of lawn, toward the splash of the pond's little fountain.

Alfie wished *her* family had a fish pond. She also wished Hanni would drop for all time the subject of Operation Kittycat, Princess, or anything else cat-related.

Not to mention the subject of her bad kitten-smuggling self.

Alfie wanted everything to be fresh and new again. After all, a week from today—at this very hour!—they'd be sitting in Mr. Havens's second grade class.

Meeting new kids.

Getting yelled at by their teacher, maybe.

Even learning something. Who knew?

"Your mom *told* you?" Alfie asked, avoiding Hanni's eyes as they settled in next to the pond to check on their fairy pathways and tiny furniture.

"Well, *yeah,* Mom told me," Hanni said. "Because she wanted to find out if I knew you didn't have permission to bring Princess home."

"Oh, no," Alfie said, freezing. "So now you're in trouble too?"

"Nuh-uh. Not really," Hanni assured her. "Because I *didn't* know. I mean, I knew you didn't want your brother to find out about Princess, or it would ruin the surprise. Only, how come you didn't tell

me about the rest of it? I wouldn't have blabbed."

"It wasn't a secret, exactly," Alfie said. "I wasn't ever trying to trick you. I was mostly thinking about how much I wanted a kitten, that's all."

"And you got busted big-time," Hanni said, her green eyes sparkling. "What happened? Are you grounded, except for this last week of the daycare club?"

Maybe I am, and maybe I'm not, Alfie was tempted to say, turning the whole thing into a joke. Because being grounded would make her sound kind of exciting and fun and interesting—to Hanni, and to the new kids in her class, wouldn't it?

That would be a pretty cool mark on her pretend whiteboard.

Hearing the Operation Kittycat story from an important class member like Hanni Sobel might change the way kids saw her. She, Alfie Jakes, could go from being known as a goofy, playful cricket to being seen as a master planner who was not afraid to come up with crazy schemes just for the fun of it.

Only Operation Kittycat hadn't really happened that way, Alfie reminded herself. She didn't begin her time in the two-girl daycare club wanting to be a sneaky kid who didn't care a bit what her parents thought.

Being a girl who didn't mind disappointing her mom and dad.

That wasn't her.

Her heart was just super lonely for a kitty.

"Did you get grounded?" Hanni asked again, sounding hungry as she waited to hear every detail of the bad news to come.

"Not really," Alfie said, shaking her head.

"But you're keeping the kitten," Hanni said, grinning. "So you got to have your own way."

"Yeah, but only kind of," Alfie said. "See, Princess belongs to everyone in the house, not just me. And she probably won't even want to sleep in my room. I'm the one who has to clean out the litter box, too," she added. "All by myself. And I can't watch TV or anything for a whole week, *and* I have to pay back the money for the stuff I borrowed from the kitchen. So I'll have *nothing.*"

"Except Princess," Hanni pointed out. "But, wow, that's really harsh, Alfie. I'm sorry. Your parents are strict," she added, shaking her head.

"I thought my mom was bad, but—"

"They're okay," Alfie protested. "It could have been a lot worse, right?"

"I guess," Hanni said, sounding doubtful.

But in Alfie's opinion, this had been a good outcome. And telling Hanni the truth—being herself, really, instead of trying to be some fake Outlaw Alfie—was another good outcome.

It was a different, better way of being new.

It was kind of a brave decision, too. But Hanni deserved the truth, Alfie decided.

And didn't a girl owe that to a new friend?

❋ ❋ ❋

The Jakes kids usually scattered after the dishes were done, but that night the whole family gathered after dinner. Princess had curled up on the fluffy blanket at the end of the family room sectional, and no one wanted to miss what this fascinating little creature might do next.

It was as if she were a tiny gray magnet drawing the Jakes family to her side. Right now, what Princess was doing was sleeping and purring at the same time. Her purr was a constant rhythmic noise, and it was surprisingly loud for such a small animal who was not much bigger than a rolled-up pair of EllRay's sports socks.

"Is that dangerous?" Alfie asked, leaning in to examine the kitten. "How does she have time to breathe?"

"I wouldn't worry about it, Cricket," her father said, stretching his long legs out carefully so as not to disturb the sleeping kitten. "But it is surprising," he admitted. He unfolded his newspaper

carefully. He clearly did not want to wake Princess with its rattle as he turned the pages. He was old school about the news, his wife sometimes teased. She preferred to keep up with current events online instead.

"Princess sounds like a motorboat," EllRay said, flopping down at the other end of the sofa. "I hope she sleeps with me tonight. I can dream I'm waterskiing."

"Maybe she'll sleep with you, and maybe she won't," Alfie said. "Because she'll probably want to sleep with *me*. That's what she's used to," she added, trying to sound as if it didn't matter to her one way or the other.

Alfie didn't want to get her mom all riled up.

"We'll be getting her a bed tomorrow or the next day," Mrs. Jakes said from the built-in desk where she paid the bills each Monday night. "Or maybe a really cute basket with a folded-up baby quilt in it. Something pretty."

"I think cats usually make up their own minds about where to sleep," her husband said from behind his paper.

"You're probably right," Mrs. Jakes said. "But it's fun making plans. And I want her to be all settled by the time school starts next Monday. A week from today," she added, not that either Alfie or EllRay needed reminding.

Mr. Havens, Alfie thought, hiding a shudder as she sat in the easy chair she liked best. It swiveled, so she could see whatever was going on in the room.

Alfie liked keeping track of things.

Well, at least she would be starting second grade with a new friend, Hanni Sobel, Alfie thought, congratulating herself. *And* she'd be "the girl with the kitten." Alfie planned on making the most of that. Nobody needed to know any of the dismal details of how Princess came to live at her house.

The stinky litter box closet.

The scratches on her legs.

The saggy curtains.

Not to mention how she'd basically lied to everyone around her.

But Princess and Hanni would be the first cool marks on her imaginary second grade whiteboard,

Alfie thought, smiling. So it was going to be a very cool year.

She *was* getting off to a good start, boy teacher or no boy teacher!

It was funny, Alfie thought, her eyes closing for a moment. Princess's purring seemed to fill the peaceful room—like bees buzzing in a summer garden, Alfie thought. Princess was like a kitten-shaped puzzle piece that had somehow completed a Jakes family portrait. They had all been missing her without even knowing it.

It was true, Alfie admitted to herself—she had imagined Princess as being devoted only to her. But like her dad said, this tiny kitty seemed to have her own ideas about what she wanted to do, and when and where she wanted to do it.

Who knew a kitten could have so many opinions?

But even though she had to share Princess, Alfie told herself, the little gray kitten was something to love.

And Alfie did love Princess—the best summer souvenir ever.

It was funny, Alfie thought, feeling drowsy in spite of the air-conditioned room. Sometimes you planned something, and it might be a really good plan. But then things turned out different from how you thought they would.

Different, but still good.

Maybe second grade would be like that, too!

Maybe having a boy teacher wouldn't be so bad after all.

Maybe meeting new kids would turn out okay.

Oh, she'd mess up again, sure. But things were going to be absolutely fine.

Alfie knew it.

Join Alfie
on absolutely all
her adventures!

* * *